Go to www.maxflash.co.uk.
and enter this code:
J3OPS11LB29
for your freebies, downloads
and other Max Flash goodies

For Mum and Dad

STRIPES PUBLISHING
An imprint of Magi Publications
1 The Coda Centre, 189 Munster Road, London SW6 6AW

A paperback original
First published in Great Britain in 2008

ISBN-13: 978-1-84715-043-1

Printed and bound in Belgium by Proost

2 4 6 8 10 9 7 5 3 1

MISSION 3

IN DEEP

Jonny Zucker

Illustrated by
Ned Woodman

MAX FLASH MISSION 3

CHAPTER 1

Max Flash vaulted over a high concrete wall
and thudded down on to the other side. He
could hear the menacing crunch of Alton's
footsteps close behind. He sprinted down a
twisting track and spotted a rope up ahead,
hanging from a wooden beam. Max grabbed at
it and started shinning upwards. Seconds later,
he swung up on to the beam and glanced back
– Alton was gaining on him.

Max darted across the top, willing himself to
keep his balance on the narrow surface. He

reached the end and looked down. The drop below was pretty steep but there was no turning back. He launched himself through the air and crashed down on to a bed of leaves, bending his knees to cushion his fall.

I've got to move faster!

Max sped off up the path, hearing Alton's feet hit the turf and come straight after him. Max quickened his pace. Up ahead were two giant oak trees with a very narrow gap between them.

I have to make it through first!

As Max thundered on, he suddenly felt a vicious stab of pain in the heel of his left foot: Alton had kicked out and struck him. Max gritted his teeth. The gap in the trees was approaching fast. Suddenly he heard a whooshing of air as Alton sprung forwards, aiming a kung fu kick at Max's head. In a split second, Max darted to his left, and then dived forwards towards the gap. As he sailed through

he heard a cry as Alton's body smashed against one of the trees.

Max skidded on his front over the ground and finally came to a stop. Slowly he got to his feet and looked round. Alton was climbing through the gap in the trees, panting, limping and looking completely humiliated.

"Good work, Max," Alton puffed. "I've been a DFEA agent for ten years, plus I designed this assault course, and you STILL beat me. You've upped your game."

CHAPTER 2

Max was about to reply when a robotic voice boomed out: "Max Flash report to Room 17 immediately." A green arrow started flashing on the wall.

"Better not keep Zavonne waiting," said Max.

Alton nodded. "Not a good idea! But watch out, Max, I'll get you next time."

Max followed the arrow to the end of the wall and rounded the corner. In front of him was a low, grey building. A black shutter lifted quickly and Max stepped inside.

He found himself in a long windowless
corridor, which had a row of numbered doors
on the left side. Max was just about to knock
on Room 17 when it silently swung open.
Inside was a rectangular, whitewashed room,
containing a metal table and two chairs.

Zavonne was seated at the table. Her hair
was scraped tightly back off her face and her
cold, clear eyes followed Max as he walked
over and sat down facing her.

He had met Zavonne before, but only as a figure on the computer screen. It was weird to see she was a human like him after all.

Zavonne worked for an organization called the DFEA – the Department for Extraordinary Activity – which dealt with "unusual" goings on that were too weird for the normal forces of law and order. Max's parents, who were stage magicians by day, had carried out two missions for the Department several years ago. Max had been recruited by Zavonne a while back, and he'd already completed two death-defying missions, one in the virtual world and one in the furthest reaches of outer space. His incredible contortionist and escapology skills honed through years of taking part in his parents' stage show had made him the perfect candidate for both of those missions.

Following Zavonne's instructions, Max had spent all day at the secret DFEA training centre, testing his physical strength to the limit. His race with Alton on the assault course had been his toughest challenge, and it had been a close contest.

"Alton's one of our fittest operatives," said Zavonne coolly, "yet you made it to the end without getting caught."

Max nodded and allowed himself a small smile – he guessed he was being trained up for his third mission, but what would it be?

"Something's come up," said Zavonne swiftly. "Way out in the Pacific Ocean is a very remote island called Decca Island. It served as a Ministry of Defence base for half a century, but two years ago the Ministry made a strategic decision to close it down. All that remains on the island is an old army barracks, a memorial statue and a lighthouse – to warn ships about the treacherous rocks surrounding the island. The Ministry is still responsible for the maintenance of the lighthouse and they visit twice a year."

Max's eyes were locked on Zavonne's as he took in every word.

"Last week," Zavonne continued, "two Ministry technicians visited Decca Island for one of these biannual lighthouse checks. As they were preparing to leave, there was a violent storm. Ferocious waves smashed on to the island, which was completely flooded. The two technicians nearly drowned as they attempted to take refuge in the lighthouse."

Max looked at Zavonne blankly. *So?*

"The Ministry concluded it was a freak storm. But the DFEA doesn't share that analysis."

"Why are the DFEA interested in some island in the middle of nowhere?" asked Max.

"The area around Decca Island is rich in sailors' tales about mermaids and sea monsters," Zavonne said. "While we at the DFEA appreciate many of these stories are just legends, we've always kept an eye on the island and the waters surrounding it."

Max blinked in surprise. *Is Zavonne sending me on a mermaid hunt?*

"So we sent a specialist marine team to investigate."

"What did they discover?" asked Max.

"Absolutely nothing," replied Zavonne, "so we instructed them to dive and investigate below the waterline."

"Did they find anything?"

Zavonne's gaze hardened. "They were less than a mile down when they were attacked."

"Attacked? By who?"

"By sharks," Zavonne nodded, "at least that's what they initially thought. It all happened very quickly and they were obviously focused on getting out of the water as fast as possible. But although the creatures coming at our men looked like sharks, they didn't move like sharks. But as I say, this was a dangerous situation and understandably the crew did not investigate further."

"Were they hurt?"

"Apart from a few cuts and bruises no one was seriously injured. But this attack on our divers and the surge of water flooding the island has set alarm bells ringing. Both incidents were hostile towards humans, which has led us to suspect some kind of USCs are living down there."

"USCs?" asked Max.

"Unidentified Sea Creatures," explained Zavonne. "We believe that these attacks are linked. We don't know who these creatures are or where they come from; we don't know what they're planning; we don't know how powerful they are. We need to find answers to these questions as quickly as possible. Any delay could spell disaster."

So what's my role going to be in all of this?

"The DFEA have spent the last few years developing a new material called Stealth Film," said Zavonne.

"What's that got to do with sea creatures and the island?" asked Max.

"When Stealth Film covers the human body," replied Zavonne, "it enables the wearer to breathe completely normally underwater without the need for an oxygen tank. Because of this, a diver covered in Stealth Film can dive much deeper than anyone using even the most up-to-date conventional diving gear. You can swim when you're wearing this Film but it also has a special weighting technology that enables the wearer to walk on solid surfaces underwater – such as rock formations and the seabed."

Cool!

"Using Stealth Film, we have created the world's first Second Skin Suit. It covers one's clothing and cannot be detected at all."

A concealed metal drawer at the side of the table suddenly opened. Inside was a garment made of wafer-thin, transparent material.

Max stared at it. "Wow! You've made all of those DFEA divers Second Skin Suits, so they can go back down and investigate these scary USCs?"

"Stealth Film is an incredibly complex material to manufacture," Zavonne continued, "and in addition, it's very, very expensive. As a result, we only had enough material for one Suit. Pick it up."

Max leaned over and pulled the Suit towards him. It unfurled and rested against his body. It was his exact size. He looked from the Suit to Zavonne and back again.

"You ... you want me to go down there?" he asked.

"One Suit – your size," said Zavonne pointedly.

"Why don't you just wait a bit longer, make some more Stealth Film and build some bigger Suits?" asked Max.

Zavonne shook her head. "First there is no time and second, there is another aspect to the Suit that fits your profile. Although we have conducted a battery of underwater tests on the Suit it is still only a prototype. The Suit has never been used in real mission conditions. Because of that, we cannot be a hundred per cent certain of its reliability."

Oh great!

"I've studied the water-based escape acts you perform in your parents' show, Max, and you have a strong ability to hold your breath under water for long periods. If the Second Skin Suit does malfunction, you will be in a better position to get up to the surface safely than any other DFEA operative."

A deep sea mission is a bit more dangerous than escaping from a water tank in Mum and Dad's stage show.

Max eyed Zavonne coolly. "I can hold my breath for three minutes underwater," he mused, "but what happens if the Suit breaks and it's more than a three minute journey to the surface?"

"I am assuming that scenario won't happen," Zavonne replied. "And after today, I'm satisfied with your fitness and stamina levels ... but make no mistake, this could be a very dangerous mission."

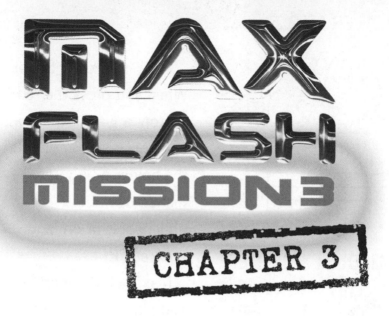

CHAPTER 3

Max looked expectantly at Zavonne. "Er, any chance of some gadgets?" he asked.

"I haven't forgotten," Zavonne replied icily. She reached down and picked up a black, metallic case from the floor. She laid it on the table and flicked open the catches. Reaching inside, she picked up a green and black marble with a tiny red button on its surface, and handed it to Max.

"There are specially concealed pockets in the Suit for your gadgets," she explained.

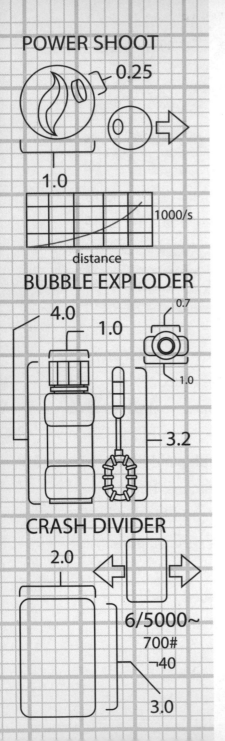

POWER SHOOT

0.25

1.0

1000/s

distance

BUBBLE EXPLODER

4.0   1.0   0.7

1.0

3.2

CRASH DIVIDER

2.0

6/5000~
700#
¬40

3.0

"This is a Power Shoot. When you press the red button, a giant explosion of compressed air shoots the holder a hundred metres upwards, underwater or on land."

Excellent!

Max took the marble and placed it in a pocket of the Second Skin Suit. Zavonne then held up a small bottle of bubbles, like the ones he'd had as a kid. She unscrewed the lid and pulled out the bubble ring. "This is a Bubble Exploder. Blow into this bubble ring and millions of bubbles are instantly released, momentarily blinding and disorientating anyone within a thirty metre radius."

She replaced the ring in the bottle and passed it over.

"And this is a Crash Divider," said Zavonne, holding up what looked like a standard football trading card.

Max turned it over in his hands.

"When you slip this between a door and its frame, or between any sort of sliding panels, it will force a narrow opening for exactly five seconds, allowing you time to get through."

Max tucked it away safely and eyed Zavonne. "So when am I going?" he asked.

"You leave tonight."

Max gulped. *Thanks for the warning!*

"Oh and one last thing," noted Zavonne.

She does have feelings after all! She's going to wish me good luck.

"Bring back the Second Skin Suit in one piece," she said, curtly.

MAX FLASH

MISSION 3

CHAPTER 4

Snub flicked a switch and the boat glided to a halt. He was a tall man, with a large chin, narrow eyes and a thick covering of stubble. He cut an imposing figure, and as the DFEA operative charged with getting Max to the start of his mission, Max hoped Snub might offer him some advice, but he was clearly a man of few words. They'd been on the boat for two hours, following a very speedy flight on a DFEA jet, and Snub had barely said anything at all.

Max touched the collar of the Second Skin

Suit, which he wore over his wetsuit. He still couldn't believe that this flimsy film was going to work. It covered his entire body yet he couldn't feel it at all. It was just like having a second skin.

"OK," nodded Snub, "very soon we reach your dive entry point. This is the place where our divers were attacked. They reported that the sharks came at them from directly below so you need to head straight down. I want you in the water quickly, so I can get the boat away without attracting attention. I will remain just outside the mission zone as directed. When you need me, pull that blue cord on your suit and I'll be with you in about ten minutes; any questions?"

Max shivered nervously and shook his head. Snub gave him an encouraging nod and started the engine. Five minutes later, he cut the motor again and gave Max the thumbs up.

This is it! No going back!

Max pulled the hood of the Second Skin Suit over his head and closed the seal. He stepped over to the edge and peered down into the watery depths, feeling a sudden stab of fear.

It's great that I've got a nice easy mission for my first ever underwater adventure!

He took a deep breath and dived.

MAX FLASH MISSION 3

CHAPTER 5

It took Max several minutes to get used to the sensation of swimming down with the Second Skin Suit on. Even though he was surrounded by water, it felt like he wasn't in the sea – he could breathe normally and the water made no impact on his body. But the amazing sights he passed reminded him exactly where he was. Here was a huge row of glowing orange anemones; there was a gigantic silver and pink fish. Although he was mesmerized by the magnificent sights, he was all too aware of what had happened to the DFEA divers. *What if a group of those weird sharks are hiding behind that rock? What if some piranhas pounce and make me their afternoon snack?*

The water changed as he dived deeper; at times it was crystal clear and then it turned muddy, restricting his vision. Deeper and deeper he went, heading past a huge shoal of long, bright-blue fish and then almost colliding with a line of swordfish, one of whom swam right up to his face for a closer inspection. He swam right through a colossal formation of yellow and black rocks, travelled for a while beside a collection of turquoise sting rays and gave a wide berth to a tight pack of spiky green fish with sharp-looking teeth.

After he'd been swimming for about half an hour, without any sign of murky goings-on, Max started to feel frustrated. Could Zavonne have been mistaken? Maybe he wouldn't find anything, however long and deep he dived.

But a few minutes later, he suddenly spotted something in the distance – it looked like a pale and distant light.

Perhaps it's an electric eel ... or a whole bunch of them!

Intrigued, Max swam on. With each stroke, the light became a fraction brighter, and a whole lot bigger, and as he dived towards it, his mouth opened in complete amazement.

It wasn't one light, it was a series of lights and as he approached he saw a high perimeter fence that stretched left and right for miles.

Max stopped and stared in disbelief. It was some kind of underwater settlement rooted to the seabed, he was sure of it. He could see buildings and carefully planted sea plants that looked like trees. But would there be anyone inside the settlement, and if so, were they the ones who attacked the other divers? Or was it completely deserted and not connected to the USCs in any way?

Max swam slowly towards the settlement, trying to take it all in. It was huge.

Time to check out the Second Skin Suit's walking in water capacity!

Max straightened up and lowered his feet on to the ground. They touched the surface and stayed put. He took a couple of steps. And then a few more. It was incredible! He was walking on the bottom of the seabed and it felt like he was walking down his local high street – the water didn't hold him back at all.

He broke into a run. *I'm going to be the world's first underwater 100 metre sprinter!*

Forcing himself to focus on the task in hand, Max skidded to a stop. He looked up at the fence, which stretched up into the distance. He could easily climb up it and swim over the top, but there were loads of powerful spotlights shining upwards. What if someone saw him? Until he could find out where he was it would be best to stay hidden.

Max walked along studying the fence, looking for the slightest weakness. A few minutes later, he found it. A small section of the fence's metal twine had come undone.

Perfect!

Very carefully, Max began to enlarge the hole, unthreading the twine until he had opened up a small gap.

He pushed his hand through to widen the hole.

The second he did this a harsh metallic beeping sounded out. *An alarm! There must be a trip wire behind the fence!*

Max stared at the fence – the gap was nowhere near the size he wanted it.

What if I rip my Suit getting through?

An automated voice started up: "INTRUDER ALERT! INTRUDER ALERT!"

There was no time to lose. Max contorted his body expertly and just managed to squeeze through.

The alarm screeched on, as did the robot warning, "INTRUDER ALERT!"

Stay around and wait for the welcoming party? I don't think so!

"INTRUDER ALERT!" shrieked the voice.

Max dropped on to the seabed on the other side of the hole and ran. Ahead of him was a series of tall, grey outbuildings. He ran past

these and then turned left into a deserted alleyway, which was flanked by high, brown walls. At the end of the alley, an archway was carved into a block of stone. Max leaned back into the stone and caught his breath.

MAX FLASH MISSION 3

CHAPTER 6

The powerful alarm voice stopped as suddenly
as it had begun. Max waited to see if it would
be activated again; it wasn't. He waited
another few seconds and peered through the
archway. Stretching to the left and right, was a
very busy thoroughfare. A huge street sign on
a high building read, MAIN STREET –
AQUATROPOLIS.

Aquatropolis!

This wasn't some tiny backwater; this was an
entire city! And it was populated by the most

dazzling array of bizarre-looking creatures, all of which were half-human, half-fish. Max could hardly believe his eyes. Some had lobster heads and human lower halves, while others had grungy human teenager top halves and swordfish bottom halves. There was even a couple with goldfish heads on top of chunky human legs dressed in lederhosen.

Unreal!

Max saw that several creatures, both male and female, with human top halves, wore colourful wraps around their bottom fish-halves.

I need one of those wraps. If I step out with a whole human body I'll stick out like a whole human sore thumb.

He watched the creatures going about their day. Some of them were swimming, others were walking, and several were just floating along. They were busy chatting, riding bikes and behaving just like humans.

*How weird is this?! It's just like a human
city, but underwater – who are these people?*

Max quickly scanned the buildings on the
street. There was a pub called The Algae &
Anemone, where a group of creatures with
salmon heads and bulky human bottom halves
were cradling huge tankards and singing
raucous songs. Further down was a glittery
steel building called the H2O Centre, outside
which a faded poster advertized a concert by
CURT AND THE WHALERS. Next to that was a
posh-looking restaurant called Le Fin.

Max looked up and spotted a giant billboard
on an advertising hoarding. It was all white
with a pair of beady brown eyes staring out,
above huge black letters:

Ray Day? Who is Ray? And what's his day about?

Max looked around, checking Main Street and the alley he'd come from. About twenty metres down was a low wall, behind which was a block of flats. There were several washing lines hanging out next to the wall. Presumably the idea behind washing lines under water was to keep clothes straight, because drying them wasn't an option. To Max's delight, he saw a line holding some wraps.

He hurried over and unpegged a blue wrap. He tied it right round the lower half of his body, making sure it completely covered his legs and feet. He checked it and checked it again.

Perfect! I'll look just like one of them. I'm just glad my friends can't see me in a skirt!

Max hurried back down the alley and stepped out into the street. He tried not to stare at some of the creatures, but it was hard when they all looked so incredibly weird. He'd come across a secret underwater race! He passed a kids' playground where two tiny toddlers with the heads of eels were whizzing down a slide.

On the other side of the playground was another poster with the eyes and the ARE YOU READY FOR RAY DAY? message. Max tried to make sense of it. This Ray guy, the owner of the beady eyes, was obviously very central to whatever was going on down here.

Where can I get some decent info? I can't exactly introduce myself to someone and say, "Hi, I'm new round here, what evil plan are you guys hatching?"

At that moment, something caught his eye. A long line of children was coming down the street. At the front was a boy with a sea bream head and a podgy, human lower half in baggy jeans and trainers. At the back was a girl with an angelic human face – complete with bright blue eyes and curly blonde hair – and octopus legs.

A scary-looking teacher, with the head of a tuna fish, was holding a clipboard and trying to keep control of the whole group. Max watched them go past and began to follow.

The teacher eventually stopped in front of a green building.

"Right then," she said in a shrill voice. "As I told you earlier, I'm standing in for Miss Rowntree today, so I don't know all of your names. But you know my name – I'm Mrs Flint. I want all of you to remember what we talked about back in class; a library is a place of silent learning, so we all need to put our talking lips – human and fish – away."

Max spotted a sign on the side of the building: Aquatropolis Central Library.

Libraries and teachers ... this is just like being at home! But at least I might find out some information about this place!

"Right 6B," trilled Mrs Flint, "let's go inside – in single file."

Max hurried over to join the back of the queue. He watched as the children at the front of the line started to shuffle in past the teacher, who ticked each one off on her clipboard. As the line went forward, the girl with the octopus legs in front of Max turned round.

"Who are you?" she demanded.

"Who are you?" Max shot back.

"I'm Harriet. I'm in class 6B. And you?"

"Er ... I'm just here for the day," Max replied.

"For one day?" she asked suspiciously.

"It's Mrs Flint," replied Max, "she's ... er ... she's ... my mum."

The girl looked from Max to Mrs Flint and back.

"Really?"

"Really." Max nodded.

"Oh. It's very uncool for your mum to be a teacher. I wouldn't mention it to the others." And with that she turned her back on him.

The queue edged forward. There were now only seven kids between Max and Mrs Flint. He quickly tapped Harriet on the shoulder. "Don't say anything to Mrs Fl— I mean, my mum. She doesn't want anyone to know."

"I won't say anything," promised Harriet.

"Right," the teacher was murmuring to

herself, as she ticked the children off her list. "Number thirty," she declared as Harriet reached her, "and that's the end of the..."

Suddenly Mrs Flint looked up. She stared at Max. "What's going on?" she enquired. "I've already counted thirty pupils in and that's the whole class. But you seem to be number thirty-one."

Max gulped.

Harriet nudged Mrs Flint with her elbow and winked at the teacher. "Don't worry," she whispered. "You don't need to pretend you don't know him. Your secret's safe with me."

CHAPTER 7

Max cringed. His cover was about to be blown!

Mrs Flint gave Harriet a funny stare. "What on earth are you talking about?" she asked.

"The extra kid; I know why he's here. He's your so—"

"I just LOVE libraries!" cried Max, treading on one of Harriet's octopus tentacles.

"Oww!" yelped Harriet.

"Yes!" Max continued. "Books are great. I love big books, small books, thin books, fat books, any kind of books."

Mrs Flint looked completely bewildered.

"He just trod on me," whined Harriet, frantically hopping about on her other seven tentacles.

At that moment there was a loud thudding sound from inside the library, as the boy at the front of the line knocked over a large table display of books. Mrs Flint groaned, placed her clipboard under her arm and hurried inside to assess the damage.

Harriet gave Max an angry stare. "I'll get you back for that," she said.

"It was an accident," replied Max.

"Yeah, right!" snapped Harriet, gliding into the building and heading over to the children's section where the rest of the class were waiting.

Max hung back, taking in his surroundings. Apart from an ancient looking sardine-faced creature that was dozing over a copy of the *Fin-ancial Times*, there was no one about.

He looked up at the signs tacked to the various sections of shelving. CORAL SCIENCE read the nearest one. He stepped between two shelves and hurried to the end of the row. He turned left, passing rows labelled NON-WATER SPORTS, SCALY HUMOUR + CARP PHILOSOPHY. He passed a table with a display of books, each with a picture of a giant purple gem on their cover, and the same title: *Tasmine Crystal.*

He hurried on and came to a sign saying DEEP SEA HISTORY. He dashed down the first row, running his finger over the titles. *Crab Archeology for Beginners, A Short History of Anemones, The Court of Lady Shrimpton.*

And then he spotted it: *Where Do We Come From? A Brief History of Aquatropolis.*

It was a slim volume with a pale-blue cover. He pulled it off the shelf and opened it. Max scanned the contents page looking for the best place to start. The title of Chapter Three caught his eye: A Reflection on our Evolution.

Max turned to the beginning of the chapter and started to read:

It is now accepted by most history experts in Aquatropolis that Humans and Slithers developed side-by-side.

So that's what these creatures down here are called. Slithers!

As Humans developed from apes, so Slithers developed from fish. The main difference between us and Humans is that in spite of retaining some ape-like features, Humans did evolve into a distinct and totally separate group of beings.

Slithers on the other hand, only evolved up to a point. We stopped at the stage where we kept a human half and a fish half. While Humans were unable to live underwater, Slithers can live on land and in water.

So these guys could come and live with us – yikes!

According to our current ruler, The Mighty King Flago, it is not fair that...

Suddenly, a hand grabbed Max roughly
by the shoulder.

He spun round. It was Mrs Flint, and she didn't look pleased.

"What under sea do you think you are playing at, young man?" she demanded in a shrill tone, grabbing him by the ear and leading him back to the children's section. "You know you can't just wander off from the rest of the class like this. And your name isn't even on the class list I was given."

"There must be some mistake," replied Max, looking round for a possible quick exit.

"Well none of the other pupils know of you and Harriet started telling me some nonsense about me being your mother." Mrs Flint narrowed her fishy eyes at him.

Max edged a few steps towards the library's exit, but the teacher caught his elbow. "No way," she said firmly. "You're coming with me. I'm going to find out who you are!"

CHAPTER 8

Max gave Mrs Flint his most charming smile.
"If you let go of me, I promise I'll tell you who I
am. There's nothing fishy going on, I assure
you," he said. *Apart from you lot!*

Max took Mrs Flint's arms and pushed her
firmly down on to one of the movable library
stools. As she opened her mouth to protest, he
put his foot against one of the legs and shoved
it with all his might. The stool sped off,
skimming over the highly-polished floor, and
taking Mrs Flint with it. The whole class burst

into peals of laughter as the teacher spun towards the children's section, knocking into books and tables and chairs as she went.

Max didn't wait to see where she ended up. He pushed open the door and sped through it back into the street. In front of him was a large shopping mall called The Reef Centre. He hurried inside. The library had been a good starting point but he needed more information. Maybe he could find a bookshop.

Then he saw a café, which had a huge TV screen in the far corner. The words ARE YOU READY FOR RAY DAY? were plastered across the screen. Seconds later, they were replaced by an image of the Earth.

Max stared up at the screen. Would he get some answers here? What did Aquatropolis's leader King Flago think wasn't fair about humans evolving to live on land and Slithers living underwater? And what did this have to do with Ray Day? Max's brain was buzzing as

he stepped into the café and walked down the central aisles. The tables were bare apart from the odd dish of mouldy-looking seaweed fritters and seaweed burgers.

Yuck! All they seem to eat in this place is seaweed!

Most of the tables were taken, but there was a spare seat at the one nearest the screen. The other three seats were taken by old Slithers with bearded human heads and prawn bodies. One of them was wearing a blue bandana and sported a large silver earring in his right ear. Their eyes were fixed on the screen.

"Is this seat taken?" Max enquired.

The men shook their heads but kept their eyes rooted to the screen. Max slid into the chair and turned his attention to the screen.

"RAY DAY will be our day," ran the commentary. "A time for conquering, a time for victory! At last we will get to use our precious Azulin Filter! At last we will..."

"To the Azulin Filter!" cried the men at Max's table, raising their glasses.

The Azulin Filter? What on earth is that? And how is it connected to Ray Day?

Max leaned forward, eagerly awaiting the next part of the commentary but the screen suddenly went blank. His heart sank with disappointment. The guys on the table turned to face him.

"So," said the one wearing the blue bandana, "are YOU ready for Ray Day?"

"Er ... yeah," nodded Max hesitantly, "totally ready – I'm really looking forward to it!"

"That's the spirit, kid!" the Slither said. "What do you think our chances are against the humans?"

Max coughed nervously. "Well ... I think ... if we fight them, er, properly, we've got a great chance," he replied.

The guys were silent for a few seconds and then suddenly, they all burst out laughing.

"Good one!"

"Imagine!" another chortled. "Six billion humans against us! We'd stand a great chance, wouldn't we!"

Other customers who'd heard Max's comment joined in with the laughter.

Max felt his cheeks redden as confusion swept through him. *So Zavonne's wrong. The Slithers aren't going to attack us. They accept*

they'd be outnumbered. So WHAT is going on?
And how am I going to find out who Ray is?

Suddenly a series of loud smashes came from
over by the bar. Everyone turned round to see
what was going on. One of the waiters had
been shoved out of the way by a hideous-
looking creature with a vicious shark head.
He'd dropped a large tray of glasses that had
crashed to the floor.

The laughter immediately stopped.

"Who's that?" Max whispered.

"Dreydor, Captain of the Shark Corp," the
Slither wearing the bandana whispered back.

The Shark Corp? Now there's a friendly-
sounding organization!

Max watched as another five of these shark
creatures stormed into the bar, fanning out
behind Dreydor and showering everyone with
accusing stares.

Dreydor took a few paces forward and
scanned the terrified faces of the café's

customers. "As you all know, an intruder entered Aquatropolis earlier today. My men and I are doing spot checks all over the city. We believe it might be a whole human."

Max gulped nervously.

"So anyone who is wearing a fashion wrap, take it off immediately," added Dreydor. "That way we can rule you out."

He paused for a second and his eyes narrowed. "Unless of course, one of you is that human, in which case we will deal with you appropriately."

Max clutched at his wrap. *What do I do?*

He couldn't just hang around waiting for Dreydor and his henchmen to make their way round the room to his table. Max glanced around, scanning his surroundings for an escape route. He wouldn't be able to get to the main entrance undetected, but there was a swing-door that led into the kitchens.

"Nothing here, Captain Dreydor!" the Shark

Corp shouted as they continued their search. They were three tables away from where Max was sitting, when he made his move. He stood up and hurtled towards the swing-door, sending everything on the table flying.

"STOP HIM!" yelled Dreydor furiously. The Captain and his troops thundered across the room after Max.

Max reached the door and threw it open. He dived through and heard it swing back and catch Dreydor in the face with a bang.

Max fled through the kitchen, speeding past a trolley on wheels and a tower of takeaway seaweed pizza boxes. He crashed through a door at the end of the kitchen and found himself in a deserted corridor at the back of the mall.

It was a service corridor stretching to his right and left. In front of him was a small goods lift. He ran over to it and thumped the button. A green light flashed. The lift was five floors above him. He hit it again but the display didn't change. *What's wrong with it!*

Behind him he heard shouting, and thudding feet getting nearer. He glanced to his left and right. He'd never make it to either end of the corridor. He was a fast runner, but these guys had legs three times longer than his. And the lift was still going nowhere.

"GET HIM!" he heard Dreydor roar.

MAX FLASH MISSION 3

Max was just starting to imagine what being eaten would be like, when he suddenly had a brainwave; the Crash Divider! It opened doors and panels! He pulled it out and slipped it between the two lift doors. In a second, the doors parted. Max dived through and immediately felt himself falling.

In his hurry to escape, Max had forgotten that there was no lift on the other side of the door! He looked down for a second – below him was a deep pit of darkness.

In desperation, Max threw his arms out, desperately searching for something to hold on to. Suddenly, his right hand found one of the lift cables. He snatched at it, gripping with all his might – just one slip and he'd be hurtling down the shaft to a certain death. His heart racing, he reached up with his left hand and held on, his legs swinging beneath him.

Above him, he could hear the muffled shouts of the Shark Corp as they arrived in the corridor to find that he'd vanished. Then he picked up the sounds of feet darting in both directions. They must have split up to hunt him down. Max breathed a sigh of relief as he swung around in the pitch-black shaft. But just as he was contemplating how best to escape, the cable he was swinging from suddenly started to move. Max looked up.

The lift! It was slamming down towards him at breakneck speed. He was about to be seriously squashed!

He could hear the high-pitched screech of the cables as the lift hurtled towards him. Up and up he flew. Down and down the lift sped. It was now less than twenty metres above him and smashing down fast.

Wincing in anticipation, Max let go of the cable and threw himself against the left-hand wall of the shaft, where there was a tiny gap.

He slid himself into the space and felt the rush of the lift as it crashed past him. But there was nothing to hold on to, and a second later Max lost his balance and toppled back into the shaft. Screaming in terror, he hurtled down the shaft for what seemed like for ever, and landed with a smack on the roof of the lift. He rolled to his side to break his fall and almost got his head cut off by a metal strut. He shook himself in disbelief as he lay on the roof, feeling the water rushing past him in the darkness.

And then suddenly, the lift started losing speed. It slowed right down and a few seconds later, it came to a halt. Max heard the sound of people getting out. He waited a few seconds and then twisted a dial on the centre of the roof. A circular panel slid open and he dropped down inside the lift. A small group of creatures with human heads and carp lower bodies were pushing a vending machine into the lift. They froze in surprise.

"Oh hi!" Max grinned, giving them a confident wave. "Problem with some cables. All fixed now."

"Let's just get this thing in," grunted one member of the group.

Max eased past them and out of the lift as they wedged the machine inside. As the doors closed he heard a Slither saying, "They're taking younger and younger staff on nowadays, aren't they? He looked like a kid."

Max allowed himself a quick grin, checked the corridors for any sign of the Shark Corp, and let himself out of the building through a glass door. He was back on Main Street, and as he stood trying to make sense of things so far he heard a commotion up ahead. A big crowd had gathered and there were excited cheers and whistles. Max hurried to see what was going on.

As he reached the crowd, he saw what all the fuss was about. A huge, cylindrical tank, with a large opaque panel on its side, was being driven down the road. People were pointing at the panel in awe. Max eased his way through the crowds until he got a clear view.

Inside the tank was a huge, purple gem, glittering and twinkling.

"The Tasmine Crystal," he heard someone utter with hushed amazement.

Max instantly remembered the display table in the library. All of those books had been about the Tasmine Crystal and now here it was. If only he'd stopped at the table and had a read – then he might have some idea what the significance of the Crystal was. Could it be related in some way to Ray Day? Was it a prize or war spoil that Ray had won?

"This is so exciting," gushed another Slither, "the Tasmine Crystal and the Azulin Filter together – what a combination!"

So the Tasmine Crystal and the Azulin Filter are connected! But how? And I'm STILL no closer to discovering who Ray is!

The crowd buzzed with excitement and moved down the road alongside the vehicle carrying the Crystal. Max was tempted to go with them and check out where the Tasmine Crystal was heading, but then he noticed that a huge trail of bubbles followed behind the tank, forming a trail to where it had come from.

Perhaps I should investigate away from the crowd...

The bubbles stretched well into the distance. It was worth a try. If he could find where the Crystal came from, it might not only tell him where it was going – it could possibly give him answers to several other questions. He looked

back down the street and saw Dreydor and his army fly out of the mall. Max checked his wrap was securely fastened round his waist and hurried away.

He didn't stop running until he was well out of the eyesight of the Shark Corp. The twists and twirls of bubbles were still strong and he followed them down several streets until they started thinning out.

Finally, Max arrived at the point where the trail had started. It was by an imposing white building with three silver turrets and a huge set of wrought iron gates. SHOAL LABORATORY read a sign on a high wall to the right of the gates.

A laboratory? I should be able to find out about the Tasmine Crystal here...

MAX FLASH
MISSION 3
CHAPTER 10

Just then he heard the loud roar of an engine. Crouching down next to the railings, he spotted a large red van approaching the gates.

Max pressed his back against the railings and watched. The van pulled up in front of the gates and a Slither with a salmon head reached out of the driver's window and pressed a switch on a small panel next to the gate.

"Delivery of Carbuncle Sodium Chlorate," the driver spoke into the intercom.

There was a pause and then the gates made

a clicking sound and started to slowly open. Max seized his chance. Crouching as low as he could, he sped over to the back of the van. By the time he reached it, it was already moving through the gates.

He scurried underneath and grabbed the exhaust pipe. He pulled himself up, stretching his body along the underside of the van and hooking his feet on either side. The engine thudded, and a flurry of bubbles hit Max in the face. He slammed a hand over his mouth to stop himself from coughing. A few seconds later the van stopped.

He heard the driver's door open and watched as two jeans-clad human legs touched the ground.

"All present and correct?" he heard a deep voice ask.

"Yeah, this is my last delivery of the day."

"Well open her up then," ordered the first voice impatiently.

Max watched as two sets of feet walked round to the back of the van. He heard a lever being twisted and then a metallic ruffle as the van's shutters were pulled open.

"It's all in there," said the second voice – the driver's.

Both sets of feet left the ground and Max heard boots climbing up on to the van's tailgate. This was followed by a scraping sound as the two creatures stepped into the van to check whatever it was that was inside. The footsteps clunked above him and he could hear muffled voices. A few seconds later the footsteps retreated and the two Slithers jumped down to the ground.

"I'm just going to get the paperwork," said the driver.

Max watched the driver's feet stroll round to the front of the van. *If I can hang on here, I might just find out what's going on!*

Max was just congratulating himself on his plan when, without warning, a strong torch beam cut through the darkness on the underside of the van. Max shrunk back in horror as the beam almost hit him.

A wave of fear snaked down his spine. He pressed himself up against the bottom of the van, desperately trying to make himself invisible as the torch beam swished first to the left and then to the right. The guard was just making a second more thorough sweep, when the driver called out.

"Can we get the paperwork done? I want a decent lunch break."

The guard paused, sighed, turned off the torch and rose to his feet. Max watched in relief as the Slither ambled over to join the driver at the front of the van. Fearing the guard might return to his torch sweep, Max quickly crawled along the pipes on the van's underside. When he reached the end, he stuck his legs out and up on to the tailgate. Pressing down very hard with his toes, he eased the rest of his body out, grabbed the tailgate with his hands, and in one swift, curled movement he flung himself up and on to his feet.

Inside the back of the van was a set of large, blue canisters – the type used to transport gas. One of them had the stopper off, and it was empty. As Max moved to investigate, he tripped over the stopper, sending it flying.

"What was that?" demanded the guard.

Max heard feet scurrying in his direction. He

flung himself forward, contorted his body and just managed to get into the canister and slam the stopper on as the guard's feet hit the tailgate again. The footsteps thudded in Max's direction. He heard the guard unscrew the stopper on another canister. And then the footsteps headed straight for his canister.

OK. The game's up. Hand me over for Dreydor's supper.

But after another agonizing thirty seconds, he felt himself being turned on to his back as his canister was lowered down on to the tailgate. Then it was rolled off the back of the van and along the ground for what seemed like for ever. Max's body spun over and over inside the canister as he felt the canister pushed over the lip of a door.

Finally, they came to a halt and he heard the footsteps retreating.

He waited; one minute, two minutes. Silence. Should he go and investigate or stay put?

Taking a deep breath, he pushed the stopper out and poked his head a fraction over the rim.

He blinked in the bright glare of spotlights. As his eyes adjusted to the light, he saw that he was in a huge, white-walled laboratory. At the far side of the room, three Slithers in white lab coats were sitting at workstations, wearing surgical gloves and punching red and yellow flashing buttons on large metallic panels fixed in front of them.

On Max's side of the lab, there was no one, just a row of shining laptops.

Keeping his eyes firmly on the lab-coat crew, he pushed himself up through the opening of the canister and lowered himself silently down its side on to the floor.

Keeping low to the ground, he crawled over to the row of laptops. He raised his right hand, reached up for the mouse and clicked it. The screen saver disappeared and the words ENTER PASSWORD appeared.

I'll just have to guess. I need to get some information on these guys!

He slid his fingers on to the keyboard and typed in RAY DAY.

INCORRECT PASSWORD flashed across the screen.

He tried AQUATROPOLIS.

INCORRECT PASSWORD the screen replied.

Next he tried TASMINE CRYSTAL.

INCORRECT PASSWORD.

Max scratched his forehead in frustration. He could be here for days and not be able to log

on. It could be any word or number or combination of both. He thought about everything he'd seen and heard since he'd been down here in Aquatropolis.

The Slithers seem to be massively in awe of their king, why not give that a go?

He typed in KING FLAGO.

INCORRECT PASSWORD the monitor bleeped back.

Max bit his bottom lip thoughtfully.

He added the words THE MIGHTY to KING FLAGO.

The screen went blank for a few seconds and Max feared it had switched itself off after his multiple incorrect passwords. But then a light-blue, watery sheen swept across the screen and the words CORRECT PASSWORD ACCESS GRANTED flashed back at Max.

Yes!

He almost shouted with relief but realized that probably wasn't a good strategy for

remaining undetected. About twenty flashing red folders now appeared on the screen. He checked that the Slithers hadn't noticed him and began to scan them quickly.

WAVE TECH.

DAILY NOTES.

LAB FINANCE.

TASMINE CRYSTAL.

Max's eyes widened. He double clicked the TASMINE CRYSTAL folder. It opened immediately and presented a large collection of individual documents. There was one that grabbed Max's attention.

It was called TAS CRYST + AQ FILT – AQUATROPOLIS CENTRAL HALL – PUBLIC PRESENTATION. Max opened the file.

The opening four paragraphs were filled with thanks to various members of something called the Ray Day Public Committee.

This looks boring and useless...

But in paragraph five things started to get more interesting and by paragraph six, he was hooked.

...Our engineers have completed the highly complex Tasmine Crystal on time. All that we needed to do now was to create the Azulin Filter. As I'm sure you're all aware, the conditions for creating the Filter happen once every ten thousand years.

Ten thousand years?

We were ready for the exact window of time when deep-sea light, current, sound and heat conditions were absolutely perfect. The process was successful and the Azulin Filter is now complete. Early

trials have been a glowing success. Linking the Filter's huge powers to the Crystal's anti-gravitational pull has produced spectacular results, even when only a tiny fraction of possible power is activated.

Anti-gravitational pull?

We therefore conclude that all is ready for Ray Day. Success is assured and our future will be bountiful and plentiful.

Bountiful and plentiful ... what?!
Max stared at the screen and racked his brains. If gravitational pull kept things down, then anti-gravitational pull must keep things up. But what things were being kept up and for what purpose? And how did this Azulin Filter link to the Crystal's pull?

Max's brain hurt with trying to work it out.
This is getting seriously scientific!

And then a thought suddenly struck him. He remembered the "freak flood" that had temporarily engulfed Decca Island.

Could it be that the anti-gravitational pull of the Tasmine Crystal pulled up water?

The report said that early trials had been a glowing success. What if the flooding of the island was an "early trial" for something much bigger? Might the linking of the Azulin Filter and the Tasmine Crystal "pull up" a far greater amount of water – an amount so large it could do permanent damage to the Earth?

He scrolled down to the next paragraph, but was interrupted by a metallic clunking sound. He looked up. The Slithers in lab coats had gone and giant steel shutters were closing over every exit.

Max leaped up and started running. His feet pounded along the shiny lab floor. The shutters were almost completely down. Increasing his speed, Max dived forward on to his knees and

turned himself into a human thunderbolt. The
smooth floor was the perfect launch pad and
his whole body flew forward at incredible
speed. In three seconds his way out would be
blocked. He leaned back as far as he could,
closed his eyes and hurtled forwards. The top
of his head missed the underside of a shutter
by a millimetre, but he was through!

CHAPTER 11

Max crashed against a wall and ricocheted off it, coming to a halt in the middle of a narrow corridor. The sound of shutters closing echoed throughout the whole building. Max turned right and sped across the white floor tiles. Twenty metres down he spotted a small skylight window in the ceiling. He pulled himself up on to a window ledge, stretched as far as he could and caught hold of the window catch. He twisted it, pushed the window open and dived through.

He found himself on a flat roof near the front
of the building. The high gates up ahead were
still open a fraction – just enough for him to
squeeze through. Checking to make sure there
was no one around, he sprinted along to the
edge of the roof and leaped down towards the
gates. But just as he reached them, a huge line
of Shark Corp heavies emerged from every
doorway.

Before any of them could take a step, Max
pulled the Bubble Exploder out of his pocket,
twisted off the screw cap, snatched the bubble
ring and blew through it.

An explosion of bubbles shot out from the
ring, straight towards the Shark Corp.

They had no time to react.

The bubbles zipped forwards, creating a
dense, swirling mass of power that flew
towards them. As the force hit them, they were
flung backwards, yelling and crashing into
each other.

Max gave the bubble ring an admiring look. *Cool!* He yanked the gates open and fled, retracing his steps back to Main Street.

I have to get back to the Tasmine Crystal. It looks like the Slithers want to use it to create a giant flood to wash us away...!

Max sped to the end of the street and turned the corner. The road ahead was empty. He sprinted down it, his feet pounding over the ground. Up ahead was another corner. He skidded round it and froze.

There in front of him were three members of the Shark Corp, blocking his path. Max quickly spun round, but to his horror three more of them stood in the road behind him. To his left others appeared from a doorway. And from the right another team of the vicious fish force emerged. He was ambushed!

And last but not least, on top of a tall building just up ahead, the hulking figure of Captain Dreydor came into view. He stepped off the building's roof, and floated down to the ground.

"Thought you were being clever with that lift stunt earlier, didn't you?" snarled Dreydor.

"It wasn't bad, was it?" laughed Max, trying to buy some time.

"Well the time for fun and games is over," hissed Dreydor.

Max swallowed nervously. What he needed was a gadget, and quickly! He reached into his pocket for the Power Shoot, but the space where he'd placed it was empty. Desperately he rooted around for it, but it had totally disappeared.

Dreydor saw Max's terror and roared with laughter.

"Come on, boys!" he declared. "It's feeding time!"

Dreydor and his men started to move in on Max, their cruel eyes locked on to him.

OK. Time's up. It's over; finished; kaput; the

end of the road. Will Dreydor feed on me and throw the leftover scraps to the others or will it be a communal feast? And what bit of me will they eat first?

As these questions zipped through his mind, Dreydor and his hideous Shark Corp had closed in. All around Max were huge jaws full of gleaming, fiercely-sharp teeth, ready to do some serious damage. He didn't stand a chance.

MAX FLASH MISSION 3

CHAPTER 12

Max closed his eyes and every muscle in his body clenched with dread.

"STOP!" a powerful voice suddenly thundered.

Max opened one eye. His head was halfway inside Dreydor's mouth.

Dreydor froze – Max could feel the Captain's teeth skimming the top of his hair.

The members of the Shark Corp bowed their heads low. "Behold the Mighty King Flago!" they chorused.

Instantly, Dreydor pulled his jaw back. Max breathed a grateful sigh of relief and looked around for the Mighty King Flago, but there was no sign of him anywhere.

And then Max's gaze fell on the ground and he spotted a tiny crab with very short, human legs and a gold crown resting on his head.

Surely, this little critter isn't the all-powerful king!

For a creature so small, King Flago did possess an impressively loud voice. "I apologize for the actions of my police force, young man," said King Flago, advancing to Max's side and looking up at him. "They do a marvellous job down here, but they can get ... how shall I put this ... a bit over-excited. This human boy means no harm," he declared, gazing round at the Shark Corp, who all still had their heads bowed.

"Our loyalties are to you, oh mighty King," whispered Captain Dreydor.

"Our loyalties are to you, oh mighty King," chorused the others.

"Excellent," smiled King Flago, "but you can leave him in my care now."

Dreydor immediately lifted his head. "Whatever you command," he stated.

'Yes," chimed the others, "whatever you com—"

"STOP REPEATING EVERYTHING I SAY!" roared Dreydor.

"Sorry, boss," a few of them muttered sheepishly.

King Flago rolled his eyes. "You will accompany me to my palace," he said to Max.

Max took a deep breath. He was sure that time was running out fast, but faced with a choice between the King and the Shark Corp, he'd take the King any day.

"Of course, King Flago," Max nodded, and grinned at Dreydor. "Nice to have met you."

Dreydor snarled but said nothing.

King Flago strode off towards the end of the street (going very slowly on account of his size) and headed round the corner, where a tiny, black stretch limo was parked.

"I would invite you in for a ride," said the King, "but I think there would be a passenger-size issue. However, my palace is big enough to house even the largest of beings and we haven't far to go."

A door slid open and Flago disappeared inside the limo. Its engine sprang to life and it pulled away with Max walking behind. He looked over his shoulder. Dreydor and his band of thugs were standing staring furiously at him.

The limo turned a corner and pulled up in front of a massive gold palace. The limo door slid open and the King emerged. Flago started to walk briskly across a gravel concourse. Max followed at the King's side, taking a quick peek behind him. There was no sign of the Shark Corp ... for the moment at least.

"We'll go straight to the banqueting room," said the King.

I need to get back to the Crystal, but a few minutes in here should be OK. And maybe Flago will fill me in on Ray Day.

Max and the King marched inside the building and across a huge, red-carpeted lobby, down a long corridor, up a set of sweeping stairs and through a grand set of double doors.

Max stopped for a second on entering the Royal Banqueting Suite. It was majorly impressive, as good as any of the pictures he'd seen of rooms in Buckingham Palace. A huge table was set with gleaming silver cutlery and covered with a white linen tablecloth.

"I hope this will be comfortable enough for you," declared the King.

"Yeah ... great," nodded Max.

The moment he and King Flago were seated – Flago on a minuscule marble throne, Max on a normal-sized gold dining-chair – a large

group of servant Slithers with human heads
and trout bottom halves swept into the room,
carrying an array of covered silver dishes. They
bowed low to Flago as they deposited the trays
on the table.

*Wow, what a feast! There must be fifty
dishes here!*

Max's eyes bulged and he felt his stomach
rumble. A quick bite to eat to give him energy
for the rest of his mission would be a good
idea...

King Flago nodded his head at the servants
and they glided out of the room as silently and
smoothly as they had entered.

"Please," nodded the King, "open as many as
you like."

Max pulled off the lid of the silver tray
nearest him. It revealed a small plate of
seaweed fritters.

*OK, OK – not a great first choice, I'll be
luckier with my second choice.*

Max prised off a second lid and discovered ... seaweed cakes. The third revealed ... seaweed kebabs. As he pulled off lid after lid his expectations faded away as did his appetite. Every single dish offered a different type of seaweed.

"Disappointing, isn't it?" remarked King Flago, fixing two very beady eyes on Max. "Unfortunately, that's all we have left down here," he explained. "The years of plenty are long gone."

"Your diet does seem a bit … limited," agreed Max.

"And it's not only food," sighed the King. "It's all of our resources. We've run dry, oh the irony!"

Suddenly Max understood. *This must be the Slithers' motivation for an assault on Earth. They have no resources left so they need to steal Earth's and the only way they can think of doing this is to flood the place by using the Tasmine Crystal and the Azulin Filter, drown humankind and then step in and bag up the necessary resources! Bingo!*

"Anyway," said the King, "tell me all about you. How did you get down here? How did you find out about us? I'm fascinated."

Max shuffled uncomfortably in his seat and eyed the room's sole exit. *I need to make a move, and soon.*

"I've always loved diving," he lied, "and this time I thought I'd go much deeper than usual."

"But you knew of our existence?"

"No," answered Max, shaking his head and glancing at the exit again. "I just ... chanced on it, you know, a lucky break."

"And who sent you?" enquired King Flago with a smiling nod of encouragement.

"No one," lied Max again. "I mean, no one official. I was on a diving trip with my family."

The King looked puzzled. "But you have no diving gear!"

"It's been lovely talking to you," said Max hurriedly, pushing his feet against the floor to stand up.

In an instant, metal clamps sprung out from under Max's chair and wrapped themselves tightly round his wrists and ankles. The chair

tilted backwards, and Max found himself lying
flat on his back, with his wrists and ankles
tightly bound.

MAX FLASH MISSION 3

CHAPTER 13

"I gave you a chance to speak the truth, human boy," yelled King Flago, hopping on to Max's chest and pointing a claw accusingly at him, "but you told me lies!"

Max flicked his wrists but the clamps held him tightly. "I'm telling you the truth," he protested.

"No you are NOT!" shrieked King Flago. "As soon as I heard there was an Earth intruder down here, I realized that trouble was afoot. The coincidence is just too great to believe!"

"Coincidence?" asked Max.

"Don't play the innocent with me!" snapped the King. "Ray Day has arrived and you just happen to chance upon us? I've never heard anything so ridiculous! The waters will be rising shortly and our great mission will be under way!"

The waters will be rising shortly! I was right! The Slithers are going to flood Earth!

"Hang on a minute," cut in Max, "Ray Day is today?"

"Don't pretend you didn't know," snarled the King. "You've seen the crowds. You've seen the Tasmine Crystal. You've even managed to get inside our laboratory!"

"OK, OK, I didn't chance on your city," said Max, changing tack. "I was sent here to explore but I swear – I didn't know anything about Ray and his famous Day."

The King leaned forward. "You are not a very convincing liar!" he declared. "Making out that

you think Ray is a creature! You reckon you're being clever don't you? Think you can fool the Mighty King Flago!"

Max's brain had gone into overdrive. *Ray isn't a creature? What have I missed? If it doesn't refer to a creature, what is it?*

"Hang on a second," said Max, trying to make sense of all of these new facts. "If you hate me so much, why didn't you just let the Shark Corp eat me?"

"And say goodbye to potentially crucial information?" sneered the King. "Not a chance! We are all set and ready down here but you may have vital news about what's happening above the surface and whether or not our human 'friends' are expecting our calling card."

"I told you," said Max firmly, "neither I nor any other humans are expecting anything. We didn't even know you existed."

Max twisted his wrists and ankles under the metal clamps.

"Is that why you sent that ship and those divers here recently?" demanded the King.

Max recalled the DFEA diving team who'd been attacked.

"We spotted them crawling all over the island," said the King darkly. "When they dived in we had to stop them – it was too risky – they might have found us and spoiled everything. So we sent them packing and hoped we'd heard the last of any reckless human explorers. And then you show up."

Why are the Slithers so concerned about the DFEA finding something on Decca Island? Think, Max, think!

"Look," said Max, "I honestly don't know what you're talking about, so just let me go and I won't trouble you again and then—"

"Let you go?" roared the King with an evil glint in his eyes. "Oh no, no, no, no! I will get information out of you. If it's the last thing you do."

Max looked up at the weedy little crab man. Flago could pinch him a bit but that would hardly hurt. It certainly wouldn't make him spill any beans on the DFEA and his mission.

Max felt reassured by this, but at that moment, Flago looked to the door and shouted, "Poison 8. I want you in here, NOW!"

CHAPTER 14

Max gulped nervously. *Poison 8? That doesn't sound like the name of a sweet and gentle creature who is going to tickle the information out of me.*

Seconds later, he heard a squelching sound and a giant monster slunk into the room. Its top half was squid-like with eight long, blue tentacles, each one ending in a glowing orange tip. Its bottom half was human and wearing combat trousers and army boots.

"Allow me to introduce Poison 8," grinned

King Flago. "Observe the orange points at the end of his tentacles. These sacs are stashed with some of the most powerful poison ever. Just one touch will send tremors of agony through your body ... but it won't kill you. My beautiful pet can inflict endless pain on his victims and as you can imagine he is very skilled at loosening people's tongues."

Poison 8 glared at Max and let out a large burp. "I'm ready, your Majesty," he announced, "just give me the word."

"Soon I will let you loose on him," cried the King, "but first a few words of instruction."

The King beckoned to Poison 8. The two of them edged towards the far side of the room and began a whispered conversation. Max got straight to work. His all time hero, Harry Houdini – the world's greatest ever escapologist – had specialized in handcuff escapes and Max had studied his methods in great detail. As the wrist and ankle clamps had snapped down on him, Max had instinctively pushed his hands and feet towards them so that they had secured themselves quite a way up his forearms and shins. Keeping one eye on the huddled conversation in the corner, he pulled his wrists and ankles towards him and silently wriggled out of the clamps.

He stared at Poison 8's tentacles. Neutralizing their poisonous threat would be tricky. Flago turned his stare towards Max. "I suggest you talk quickly," he snapped, "that way you will avoid a marathon of pain!"

And with that the tiny crab King bustled out of the room. Max gulped. If Poison 8 took even the quickest look, he would see Max was free from the clamps.

I have to keep his eyes on me.

"Poison 8," said Max staring deep into the squid man's eyes. "Perhaps we could come to some sort of arrangement?"

Poison 8 belched. "I shouldn't have had those seaweed burgers," he muttered.

"I have to say, Poison 8, your tentacles really are impressive."

"Don't try and flatter me," replied Poison 8, moving closer, but he did seem to like the compliment. "The Mighty King Flago has told me what he needs from you and I will follow his command to the letter."

"Sure," smiled Max, "I understand, but there is something you ought to know about the Mighty King Flago. He told me a couple of quite uncomplimentary things about you."

"I don't believe you," retorted the giant squid, but he was beginning to look confused.

It was the break Max needed. With incredible speed he leaped off the chair and grabbed one of Poison 8's tentacles just above the orange tip. In a maze of swirling arm movements, he tied the tentacle up with the seven others and stood back to admire his handiwork.

Poison 8 tried to scream but all that came out was a tiny whimper.

"I'll hopefully not be seeing you around," said Max, hurrying across the room to the door, "but if I see the King I'll send him your kindest regards."

MAX FLASH MISSION 3

CHAPTER 15

Max sped out into the corridor. He saw a
servant up ahead but she turned left and
disappeared through a doorway. Max set off,
thankful that he'd memorized the way he'd
come in. He made it back to the stairs leading
down to the lobby without seeing anyone, but
two servants were standing in the lobby
entrance deep in conversation.

Max looked round and spotted a large vase
of pink flowers. He grabbed it, and threw it
over the banisters, to the far right-hand side of

the lobby and ducked out of sight. The vase crashed on to the red carpet, sending shards of glass and pink flowers everywhere. The servants spun round, saw no one and hurried over to clear up the mess. Max sped down the stairs, scurried across the lobby and out of the palace.

The street outside was chaotic, with alarms sounding and Slithers running in every direction. A huge searchlight beamed out over the whole of Aquatropolis, hunting him down. *So much for being undercover!*

As Max watched the light it suddenly hit him. *That's it! Ray Day must refer to a ray of LIGHT. That's why the Slithers were worried about humans snooping around Decca Island – because of its lighthouse! They must have used it somehow for the initial flooding experiment, which means the Tasmine Crystal and Azulin Filter must be on their way there now – I must hurry!*

His thoughts were just going into hyperdrive when they were shattered by a deafening roar.

"SEIZE HIM!"

Max spun round. To his horror, the Shark Corp and Dreydor were a short way down the street. And this time they had wheels. Each of them was on a huge, silver motorbike and they were gunning straight for him, with Dreydor at the head of the pack.

When Dreydor's bike was almost upon him, Max dived to the side. The bike swerved violently, throwing Dreydor into the middle of the road. He thudded to the ground and his bike crashed on to the road beside him.

Max didn't waste a second. He ran over, hauled up the bike and leaped on to it, twisting the throttle to activate the jet propulsion. The bike lunged forward and Max performed an unplanned, but spectacular wheelie. He looked up to see a row of sharks, revving their engines and snarling in fury.

The chase was on!

Max urged the bike forwards, making a beeline for the surface. Beneath the roar of the bike's engine, he could hear the spluttering roars of the engines behind him. Max took a quick look over his shoulder. He had about twenty metres on them.

He had to make it to the surface and stop their Tasmine Crystal plan, whatever it was. Up and up through the water he sped, relieved to see that he was keeping his lead. He kept on giving the bike

nudges and making turns to try and shove the Shark Corp off his tail, but they were rock steady in their pursuit. They meant business.

As Max rode higher, the sights of plant and fish life began to rush past him. He sped past a giant yellow and red coral and a shoal of silver fish. He ploughed on.

I must be getting near to the surface.

But still there was no sign of the waterline. And then Max heard an engine roar unlike the others. This one sounded like a massive speed boat. Max looked back and his heart leaped with fear. It was Dreydor, this time riding an enormous orange and silver quad bike that was much more powerful and speedy than the Shark Corp's bikes. And he was catching Max.

Max hit the throttle again and his bike lunged forwards, but it made no difference – Dreydor was still closing the gap on him and by the look on his face he hadn't quite forgiven Max for not becoming a tasty snack.

Desperately, Max weaved left and right, darting here, shooting there, trying to shake off Dreydor. But he was no match for the Captain's high velocity bike and he felt a sickening thud as the front of Dreydor's bike nudged the back of his...

NO!

Max's bike spun left, nearly knocking him off. As he righted himself, Dreydor drew parallel with him, a huge grin plastered across his face. In panic, Max kicked out, his leg smashing against the side of the Captain's bike. But it had as much effect as a butterfly wing. Dreydor howled with laughter, showing his terrifying set of teeth.

Come on, come on, think of a plan or you'll be fish food!

Suddenly, Max spotted a large rock formation up ahead. He gunned the throttle and rode straight towards it. But at the last minute he slammed his bike to the right, clearing the rocks by millimetres. The rocks took Dreydor by surprise, but instead of smashing into them, he veered round the other side.

As Max emerged at the far end of the rocks, Dreydor appeared on the other side, grinning with the scent of victory. Max racked his brains. *What would Harry Houdini do in a situation like this?* It was a stupid question. Houdini had never been on an underwater motorbike being chased by a gruesome half-shark, half-human madman.

Just as Max began to despair, he looked up and spotted it ... the surface! It was still some way off but he was getting close. Full of excitement and relief, he took his eye off Dreydor for a couple of seconds leaving himself open to attack. Dreydor reached out and grabbed Max's right shoulder. Max pulled to the left, and as his bike skimmed off in the other direction, Max broke away from

Dreydor's grasp. But as he did so he heard a strange ripping sound.

He looked down at his shoulder and, to his horror, saw a large tear in his Second Skin Suit. Before he had a chance to assess the full extent of the damage, water suddenly gushed into his lungs.

MISSION 3

CHAPTER 16

Disaster! The rip had broken the breathing
mechanism of the Suit. He had no oxygen!
Immediately he closed his mouth and his nose,
swallowing a fair amount of water in the
process. In the madness of the moment,
Dreydor struck again. He leaped off his bike
and grabbed Max by the throat, a thin smile
appearing on his face.

Max realized instantly what the captain was
doing. *He's going to keep me down here until
I drown!*

Max glanced back and saw the other bikes approaching – Dreydor's army had arrived.

Zavonne had said that Max's ability to hold his breath underwater could come in handy, but he could only manage three minutes.

Any more than that and I'll be history!

There was no way he was going without putting up a fight. Max gritted his teeth and gave Dreydor a hard punch on the nose.

Dreydor let out a high-pitched yelp of pain and let go of Max, who somersaulted through the water and landed on Dreydor's floating bike. He cranked the throttle and the bike flew forward. Max grabbed the handlebars and directed the bike up, straight for the surface. He knew he had very little time to get there. His breath was holding, but he was beginning to feel pressure in his lungs.

Dreydor and the Shark Corp pelted after him. *I can't hold my breath for much longer!*

Max could feel himself getting weaker, but the shimmering surface beckoned and with one last mighty push, the bike spat forward and crashed out of the water.

It flew up into the air taking Max with it. Max let go of the handlebars and tumbled through the air before he landed with a crash back in the water. He plunged down beneath the surface and saw Dreydor and his heavies heading straight for him.

Max turned and swam back up to the surface, kicking frantically. As he broke through, he saw the dark black sky, with its sheet of silver stars. And there, about a hundred metres away, was Decca Island. He took off in a furious front crawl, desperate to reach dry land. He heard gigantic splashes behind him as the other bikes sped out of the water, their riders suspended in mid-air for a second before crashing back into the ocean.

Max swam on. He reached the sloping bank of jagged rocks in front of the island and scrambled out of the water. As he grabbed at the rocks and dragged himself clear he took a quick peek back – the Shark Corp were powering their way towards him.

Max took off across the rocks. Stretching up above him was the lighthouse, with its rotating beam of light at the top. As he stared up he lost his footing and slipped, gashing his knee – but he steadied himself and pushed on.

On and up Max climbed and as he neared the top of the rocks he spotted something that made his heart leap with fear. On the other side of the lighthouse the Tasmine Crystal was sat on top of a steel pole. It was suspended a hundred metres in the air, held in place by a troop of sharks, who were stationed in the water below. The Crystal's sides glittered in the moonlight. It looked like a giant orb of purple fire.

Max saw at once that it was the exact same height as the rotating light in the lighthouse. But the light shining out from the lighthouse wasn't an ordinary beam. It was a deep shade of bright violet.

The Slithers must have already attached the Azulin Filter ready for Ray Day! I've got to hurry – the completion of my mission is so very close!

CHAPTER 17

Max upped his pace and ran as fast as he could over the carpet of jutting rocks, towards the lighthouse door. He looked up and saw that the light had begun to slow down.

When the Azulin Filter shines the light on to the Crystal it must activate the anti-gravitational pull – I have to knock the beam off course!

Max grabbed the door handle and gave it a twist. It was firmly locked. He barged his shoulder against it, but there was absolutely no movement. He looked upwards again. The lighthouse light was now almost stationary.

"STAY AWAY FROM THE LIGHT!" screamed Dreydor, scrambling over the rocks behind him.

But Max was in no mood to obey any command from the freakish shark-head. He hurried round the side of the lighthouse and spotted a long black metallic ladder that rose right to the top. Max sprung on to the first rung and began to climb. Above him, the light with its eerie violet glow was grinding to a complete standstill, preparing to hit the Tasmine Crystal.

Max sped upwards but he was running out of time. The special filtered light from the lighthouse stopped and its immense ray of violet light hit the Tasmine Crystal full on. The Crystal's surfaces lit up shooting sparks of light down towards the water.

No!

Max grabbed the next rung and hurried on.

The waters below the Crystal were starting to froth and make a fearsome whooshing sound. Seconds later, the water began to rise into the air.

The anti-gravitational pull! It's started!

And this wasn't just a few little drops of water. This was the most enormous surge; a massive, ever-increasing vortex of water was streaming upwards. And it kept on coming.

"YOU WILL NOT STOP RAY DAY!" screamed Dreydor.

Max looked down. Dreydor was powering up the ladder behind him and there were five other Shark Corp guys further down. Max heard a click as a bolt just below him broke away from the lighthouse wall. Another click sounded and two bolts above him came away and fell to the ground. There was far too much weight on the ladder.

It's going to come unstuck and take us all with it!

There was a series of clicks and pops as nuts and bolts started raining down. Max looked out to sea. The massive tide of water was still rising in the air, growing bigger and bigger. When it crashed back down, the land would be completely submerged! The ladder was now swaying dangerously from side to side as it was ripped further and further off the wall.

Max pushed on; he was now only a few metres from the light. As he reached the top, he pulled himself on to a slim ledge. The floor was very slippery and coated in grease. Max crawled towards the circular drum of metal that held the light.

I have to stop the ray's focus on the Crystal!

The mass of water was rising fast and at its peak it was already hundreds of metres high. Max took hold of the metal drum and tried to twist it. There was absolutely no give – it was firmly rooted to the spot. He tried again but it didn't budge.

"I COMMAND YOU TO HALT!"

Max looked round. Dreydor was half sliding, half crawling towards him.

Again, Max tried to move the drum, but it was no good.

I have to shift the ray, I HAVE TO!

"Give up," hissed Dreydor. "You've tried and failed. Come away from the light. I won't hurt you. Trust me."

Max gave a short and bitter laugh. "I trust you less than your weedy, lying King," he snapped.

"How dare you insult the Mighty King Flago!" roared the Captain.

But Max had no time for an argument. He'd just spotted something. There on the surface of the drum was a tiny oval opening, just big enough for him to squeeze through.

He grinned as he contorted himself and slipped inside the drum, relishing Dreydor's howl of horror. He knew he was running out of time to set the light off-course before the vortex of water grew too powerful. He threw his whole weight against the side of the drum. There was no movement.

Come on! Earth will have the biggest bath in history if you don't do something!

Max gritted his teeth and, summoning up every single ounce of energy he possessed, he slammed his whole body against the side of the drum. There was a slight creaking noise and the drum cranked the tiniest fraction to the left...

Do it again!

Max threw himself at the wall again.

This time, with a groan, the drum shifted several centimetres ... and the beam of light moved a fraction more.

With the light not completely shining on the Tasmine Crystal, its anti-gravitational pull was broken. The gigantic sheets of swirling water suddenly stopped in mid-air and began to

retrace their steps.

"NOOOO!" bellowed Dreydor, from outside the drum.

But it was too late. The water that had been heading so forcefully upwards was now smashing back down – it was going to pulverize the lighthouse.

Max had to move fast!

MAX FLASH MISSION 3

CHAPTER 18

Where was the Power Shoot? Max reached again into the pocket of his Second Skin Suit and rooted around – to his joy he felt the green and black marble in the lining.

The DFEA really need to employ some better tailors! He pressed the tiny red button on its surface. As the water hurtled down towards the top of the lighthouse, Max was shot a hundred metres up into the air. As he hovered there, he could see Dreydor and all of the Shark Corp being thrown over the rocks and tossed back into the ocean.

As the water hit the Tasmine Crystal, it shattered into thousands of fragments, which rained down into the sea. The steel pole that had been holding the Crystal sunk, as did the Shark Corp who had been holding it up.

Max remained perched in the air as the water continued to rain down. But as he watched the flow of water begin to subside, the effects of the Power Shoot wore off and he dropped down into the ocean below.

He hit the water and sunk downwards. With some powerful leg strokes he kicked back up to the surface and trod water as he reached for the blue chord on his Second Skin Suit. Snub

would be here in ten minutes.

As Max floated he kept on checking the waterline for signs of the Shark Corp. But the waters were clear and he saw no menacing shapes about to break out. Very slowly, although he was neck deep in cold water, he began to relax a bit.

I did it! The lab computer had said the conditions for creating the Azulin Filter occurred once every ten thousand years. The Slithers would have to wait a long time to try and pull a stunt like this again.

Max floated calmly listening out for the sound of Snub's approaching boat. Suddenly, without warning, something clasped his feet, and he felt himself being dragged downwards. His head dipped under the water and he instantly began to hold his breath. He looked down. Holding on to his feet with a more crazed look than ever was Dreydor.

"Thought you'd got away with destroying

Ray Day, did you?" snarled the captain, his eyes burning with hate.

Max was about to reply, but remembered he'd get a huge lungful of water if he spoke so he just shook his head.

'Say goodbye to the world, human boy!" cackled Dreydor.

Max anticipated the snarling Slither's next move. Dreydor lunged up and opened his huge jaws, preparing to bite Max's head off but Max was ready. As Dreydor's teeth flew towards him, Max reached out and grabbed something floating beside him in the water. It was a chunk of the Tasmine Crystal. He stuffed it into the Captain's mouth just as his jaws snapped shut. Dreydor howled in agony.

Max took advantage of Dreydor's pain and aimed a powerful kung-fu kick at his stomach. The Captain howled again and shot downwards into the murky depths. Max gave him a quick goodbye wave, and kicked up to the surface.

As his left hand shot through the water he felt a strong grip pulling him up.

Not another Shark Corp heavy!

Bu the grip belonged to Snub, who yanked him out of the water and over the side of the boat. Max fell on to the boat's floor.

"Let's get out of here!" Max croaked.

Snub didn't need telling twice. He pulled at the engine cord and the boat shot off into the night. As it sped away from the island, Max heard Dreydor's frenzied whine of defeat.

"What was that?" asked Snub, looking at Max with amazement.

Max took a deep breath and sat up. "OK," he began, "right at the bottom of the sea, there's this amazing city called Aquatropolis..."

MISSION3

Zavonne stared frostily out at Max from the plasma screen in the operational room below the Flash family's cellar. She had spent the last hour debriefing him in minute detail about his experiences in the depths of the ocean.

"And you're sure about the Slithers not being able to repeat this plan?" asked Zavonne.

"They could build another Tasmine Crystal, but it won't be any use if they don't have this. In fact, they'd have to wait ten thousand years to make another one!"

Max reached into his pocket and pulled out the Azulin Filter. He'd snatched it just before the cascades of water had hit the lighthouse.

Zavonne gazed at it in silence.

OK. Maybe, just maybe, I'm going to get some praise!

A metal drawer on the wall began to flash.

"Open it and place the Azulin Filter inside," Zavonne said.

Max walked over, opened the drawer and gently placed the Filter inside.

"Now close it," demanded Zavonne.

Max followed her instruction.

Zavonne was silent for a few seconds. "Your parents must be pleased at your safe return."

Max nodded. After hugging the life out of him, his mum and dad told him they wanted to hear every single detail about the mission, after his debrief with Zavonne.

"There is however, an issue of great concern to me," noted Zavonne curtly.

Come on, Zavonne! I've just stopped the Earth from being totally washed out. Don't tell me off for anything!

"It's the Second Skin Suit," said Zavonne. "I did tell you to bring it back in one piece."

Is she for real?

"Yes," replied Max defensively, "but you didn't know I'd be facing Captain Dreydor and the Shark Corp."

"True," mused Zavonne, "but repairing the Suit will be a very costly and time-consuming exercise."

"It was ripped in the course of action," Max pointed out. "There was nothing I could do about it."

Zavonne considered this for a few seconds. "I won't labour the point," she declared, "I just want to remind you to be extra careful when using DFEA materials."

"Yes, Zavonne," answered Max sulkily.

"Right then," she said in a brisk, business-like fashion. "Our paths may well cross again soon."

Max didn't get a chance to reply. The image of Zavonne disappeared and the screen went blank.

At dinner, Max went into every detail of his mission, just as he'd promised his parents. After the meal, his dad got up to start the washing up.

"We dealt with Mutant Sandmen," said his mum, with a smile, "but the Shark Corp sound a lot more fierce."

"They are," replied Max, "and they're still down there."

"Well at least they won't be trying to flood

the Earth again," said his dad.

"Yes," nodded his mum. "Keeping the Azulin Filter was brilliant. We're really proud of you."

At least someone appreciates me!

His dad flung a tea towel in his direction. Max caught it and looked at him in shock.

"You're not serious, Dad?"

"What?" his dad laughed. "Let you off drying up duty because you've defeated the Slithers? No chance!"

Max grimaced and picked up the first plate.

I've just managed to save the world from a watery grave and my reward is to dry up? How outrageous is that?

EPILOGUE

Down in Aquatropolis, the Mighty King Flago had just given Captain Dreydor the most immense ear-bashing of all time. He sat alone in the palace banqueting room. The doors opened and a line of servants entered, carrying a selection of silver trays. They came to a stop and placed the trays down on the table. The King didn't move.

The head waiter gave a nod and the servants pulled off the tray lids in one swift movement. King Flago let out a shriek and banged his claws on the table.

"I HATE SEAWEED!" he yelled.

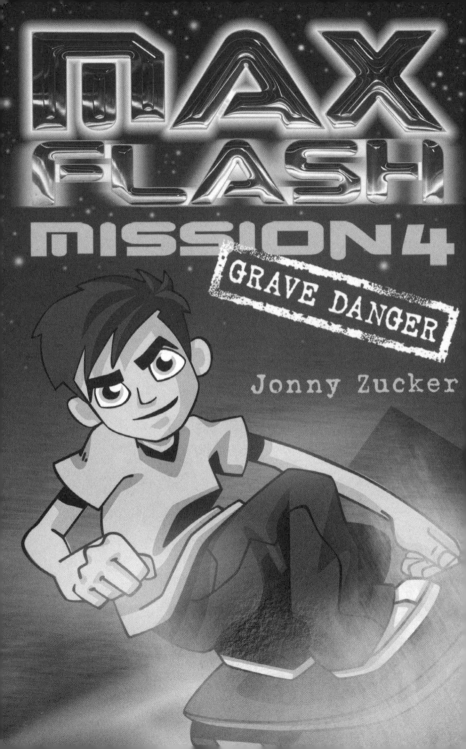

JOIN MAX ON HIS NEXT AMAZING MISSION: GRAVE DANGER, HITTING BOOKSHOPS IN JULY 2008.
SEE YOU THERE!